DISCARDED

Mean Old Uncle Jack

Anna Grossnickle Hines

CLARION BOOKS · NEW YORK

For Jack, who dared me to do it.

The full-color art was prepared in colored pencil.
The text type is Palatino.

Clarion Books
a Houghton Mifflin Company imprint
215 Park Avenue South, New York, NY 10003
Text and Illustrations copyright © 1990 by Anna Grossnickle Hines

Library of Congress Cataloging-in-Publication Data
Hines, Anna Grossnickle.
Mean old Uncle Jack / Anna Grossnickle Hines.
p.   cm.
Summary: Uncle Jack loves to tease the kids with scary mean faces
and growly mean noises, but one day his nieces and nephews turn the
tables on him.
ISBN 0-395-52137-8
[1. Uncles—Fiction.]   I. Title.
PZ7.H572Me   1990   89-17398
[E]—dc20   CIP
                                         AC

WOZ 10 9 8 7 6 5 4 3 2 1

Uncle Joe just says hello
and Uncle Dan will shake your hand,

but don't turn your back
on Uncle Jack.

Look out for mean old Uncle Jack.
He makes scary mean faces.
He makes growly mean noises.

He hides around corners.
He sneaks under tables.

You never know where,
you never know when,

he might pounce!

And then,
when he gets you,

he rubs you with whiskers.

He rumples your hair.

He grabs you and tickles
and tickles
and tickles.

Uncle Jack shows no mercy.
Uncle Jack doesn't care
if you scream and you wriggle
and holler and squirm.

You can try to sneak by.
You can try to creep by.

But old Uncle Jack
has eyes in the back,

and he'll get you,
he will,
if you try.

He might butter your nose
if you dare to sit close.

Or he'll sneak up behind you
and buckle your knees
with a bump.

Oh, he's bad, bad, bad, Uncle Jack.

SHHHHH! Don't say a word!

Don't make a sound! Because...

Old Uncle Jack is taking a nap.

ATTACK!

We've got him!
We've got him!
We'll make scary mean faces.
We'll make growly mean noises.

We'll tickle and tickle
and rumple his hair.

They got you, Jack.

Yaaah!

We'll show him no mercy.
We won't care
if he screams and he wriggles
and hollers and squirms.

We've got him,
we have,
and now…

Now we'll all give him hugs,
because that's what he likes.